DRAGON and MONSTER TALES

retold by
Corinne Denan

illustrated by
Jennie Williams

Troll Associates

Library of Congress# 79-66329
ISBN 0-89375-326-2/0-89375-325-4 (pb)

CONTENTS

The Mysterious Knight

Long ago, in a faraway kingdom, there lived three handsome Princes. The King and Queen loved them all and were very proud of them. They dreamed that the Princes would grow up and do very princely things, such as fighting duels and ruling the kingdom.

The older sons were happy to do as their parents wished. But the youngest Prince said, "I care only for the woods. I shall be a forester and nothing else."

The Queen was dismayed, and the King was furious. It did not seem proper for a person of royal blood to become a common forester. But nothing would change the young Prince's mind.

One day the King and the youngest Prince had a rather noisy quarrel over this matter. In a fit of temper, the King said, "If you must be a forester, then *be* one—but not in *my* royal kingdom. I banish you from the realm!"

"Very well, Father," said the Prince in his most haughty manner. But, in truth, he was quite frightened at the thought of being banished.

The young Prince kissed his mother the

Queen, put on a green suit of forester's clothes, and left the realm.

He soon discovered that it is one thing to dream about doing something, and quite another to actually *do* it. No one wanted to hire him as a forester, because he had no experience. Soon he grew cold and hungry and very sad.

The Prince sat under a tree to think about what he should do. Before long, he fell asleep. And when he awoke, he saw a tall stranger standing before him.

They took a liking to each other, and it wasn't long before the stranger invited the Prince to share his little house in the woods. The Prince stayed there for a number of years, and they became close friends.

Now it happened that in that part of the world, there lived a very fierce, fire-breathing Dragon. Every year, the Dragon demanded a gift of two sheep and one human being. The King of that land had decided that the fairest way to choose the human was to draw lots.

This year, as always, the drawing was held on the castle steps. But to everyone's surprise, the person who was chosen to be eaten by the Dragon was the King's daughter! Everyone in the land thought this was most unfortunate. Especially the Princess. But the drawing was fair, and no one could think of a way to change it. The Princess would have to be left in front of the Dragon's cave the very next morning.

"I must find a way to save the Princess," the Prince said.

"There is only one way," said the Prince's friend. "Take this ring and this wand. Tomorrow morning, you must turn the ring on your finger. You will find yourself in the castle of a giant. Use the wand to overcome him. Take the key from his pocket. Do with it as you will. Then take his sword and his horse. Turn the ring again, and you will be standing between the Princess and the Dragon's cave. To save the Princess, you must slay the Dragon with the giant's sword."

"Thank you, my friend," said the Prince. Then he turned the ring, and found himself in a huge castle. Before him stood a terrible giant.

"You miserable wretch!" roared the giant.

The Prince swung the wand, and the giant toppled to the ground. Then he took an iron key from the giant's pocket, and opened an iron chest. In the chest was a suit of armor. The Prince dressed himself in the armor, and at once

became a Knight of Iron. He took the giant's sword and horse, and then he turned the ring again.

At once the Mysterious Iron Knight stood between the Princess and the Dragon's cave. The Knight called out in a loud voice, "Come out here, Dragon. If you want the Princess, you must fight for her."

"Not today," the Dragon called back. "Perhaps tomorrow."

So the Princess went back to her castle, and the Knight of Iron rode off into the woods. The next morning, when the Prince awoke, he saw that the horse, the sword, and the iron armor were gone.

"Turn the ring again," said the Prince's friend.

The Prince turned the ring, and there in front of him stood a second giant, more terrible than the first. The Prince swung the wand, and the giant toppled to the ground. He took a silver key from the giant's pocket, and opened a silver chest. In the chest was a suit of armor. The Prince dressed himself in the armor, and at once became a Silver Knight. He took the giant's sword and horse, and then he turned the ring again.

At once the Mysterious Silver Knight stood be-

11

tween the Princess and the Dragon's cave. The Knight called out in a loud voice, "Come out, Dragon. If you want the Princess, you must fight for her."

But the Dragon called back, "Not today. Perhaps tomorrow."

So once again, the Princess went back to her castle and the Knight rode off into the forest. And the next morning, when the Prince awoke, he saw that the horse, the sword, and the silver armor were gone.

"You must turn the ring once more," said the Prince's friend.

So the Prince turned the ring a third time and found himself staring at a third giant more terrible than the other two. He was so tall and broad that there seemed to be no end to him.

The Prince hit the giant in the ankle with the wand, and the giant stumbled and fell to the ground with a crash. The Prince took a golden key from the giant's pocket, and unlocked a golden chest. Inside was a suit of armor. The Prince dressed himself in the armor, and at once became a Golden Knight. He took the giant's sword and horse, and then he turned the ring again.

Now the Mysterious Golden Knight stood between the Princess and the Dragon's cave. And

the Knight called out, "Come here this instant, Dragon. I have waited long enough!"

First there was silence. Then the earth began to tremble. The sky grew dark. Then, with a noise like a great clap of thunder, the Dragon rushed out of its cave. The Princess was terrified. Even the Golden Knight grew pale. The hideous Dragon had seven heads. And each head breathed long tongues of fire. Great hissing noises came from its nostrils. Its skin was green and slimy. And there were snakes and toads all over its body. The dragon was truly a loathsome sight.

But the Knight sat bravely upon the horse, holding the mighty sword of the mighty giant. The great Dragon charged, and the Knight raised the sword. The horse pranced this way and that, dodging the Dragon's seven heads. The Knight felt his arms grow weak. He could not last against this mighty beast.

Just then, the horse began to charge straight at the Dragon. The Knight felt new strength flow back into his tired arms. Raising the great sword above his head, he swung at the Dragon with a mighty blow. And all seven Dragon heads fell at once!

Then a great cheer went up across the land.

The Princess had been saved by the Mysterious Knight. The people began to dance and shout in the streets. In all the confusion, the Knight slipped away, and rode off into the forest.

When the Prince awoke the next morning, he saw that the horse, the sword, and the golden armor were gone.

The King and the Princess looked all over the land for the Mysterious Knight. But he was nowhere to be found. This made the Princess very sad, for she had fallen in love with him.

When the Prince heard of the Princess' love, he took his harp to the castle and played for her. He played such lovely music that everyone, including the Princess, was enchanted. Then he told her that he was the Mysterious Knight who had slain the Dragon.

They decided to marry, and preparations began at once. A great wedding was held in the banquet hall the very next week.

Right in the middle of the wedding feast, the Prince's friend arrived, and said, "I have come to ask a favor of you."

"Name it, and it shall be yours," said the Prince. And he told the King and the Princess of all the things his friend had done to help him.

Then the friend drew his sword and handed it

18

to the Prince, saying, "Take my sword and cut off my head."

All the people gasped, and the Princess turned pale. The Prince replied, "I cannot do such a thing, my friend. I owe everything to you. I cannot kill you in return."

"You have promised to grant me one favor," said the friend, "and you must keep your promise."

Slowly, the Prince took the sword. He drew a deep breath. Then, with one great swing, he cut off the head of his friend.

And there, before the astonished eyes of all, stood a handsome lord. He bowed low before the Prince and the Princess.

"I am the lord of a faraway land," he said. "Many years ago I was traveling in this country, and a spell was cast upon me. It could be broken only when I found a friend who was courageous enough to slay a Dragon and then take my life."

After that, the feasting and merrymaking went on for three full days. Everyone was happy that the Dragon was dead, that the enchantment was broken, and that the Prince and Princess were married. And, of course, everyone lived happily ever after—especially the Prince, who spent his days taking special care of the woods and forests.

Gavin and the Dragon

Many, many years ago, a dreadful monster came out of the North. It was the most terrible Dragon that had ever walked the earth. Its body was that of an ox and its legs those of a frog. Its long, lashing tail stretched out behind it farther than the eye could see. The scales that covered its body were so thick that nothing could break through them. Its huge, burning eyes were so blinding that people almost willingly walked into its hideous, gaping mouth.

Wherever the terrible Dragon went, the land was laid bare. One day, the King of a peaceful land learned that the Dragon was at the edge of his Kingdom. Everyone was terrified—especially the King's beautiful daughter. So the King offered a handsome reward to anyone who could slay the Dragon. Many knights were brave enough—or foolish enough—to try. But each one was quickly eaten.

Finally, the King called his council together. "What can we do to rid ourselves of the Dragon?" he asked.

No one said anything for a long while. Finally,

a very wise old man spoke. "I have heard of a magic ring," he said. "Engraved upon it is a message that reveals the only way the Dragon can be overcome. But alas, I have not the slightest notion where the magic ring may be."

A poor young man named Gavin said that he would find the ring and slay the Dragon. But the King and the council members only laughed. How could a poor youth succeed where many bold knights had failed? "Yet if you can do what no others have done," said the King, "I shall grant you any three wishes."

So, Gavin began his search for the magic ring. He traveled to many lands, but could find nothing.

One day, Gavin met a magician. "I do not know where the ring is," said the magician. "But if you could speak the language of the birds, I am sure they would tell you how to find it."

Then the magician taught the young man the language of the birds. After that, he sent Gavin on his way, saying, "When you find the ring, bring it back to me, and I will read the message for you. No one else will understand it."

And so it was that one day, as he was resting under a tree, he heard a bird say, "That young fool below wanders about looking for the magic ring."

"Only the Witchmaiden can tell him where it is," said another bird.

Then the first bird said, "Every month when the moon is full, she comes to bathe in the stream."

"The moon will be full tonight," the second bird said. "Let us fly to the stream."

Gavin saw the birds fly away, and he followed them. At last, tired and out of breath, he stopped at a small clearing. In the middle was a cold, clear stream. The young man sank to the ground beside a huge tree and fell asleep.

When he awoke, the moon was shining down upon the clear water. Suddenly, Gavin heard a slight rustling in the wood, and out stepped the Witchmaiden. He could not take his eyes from her, and he sat unmoving, hardly daring to breathe.

Not looking to the right or left, the Witchmaiden knelt down by the stream and washed her face nine times in the clear water. Then she looked up at the moon and walked nine times around the stream.

Suddenly, she saw Gavin sitting under the

tree. "I do not like being spied upon," she said. "What business have you at this place?"

"I am but a poor wanderer," said Gavin. "Quite by accident, I found this spot."

The Witchmaiden's eyes flared, and then a strange smile crossed her lips. "Come with me to my castle," she said. "It is far more comfortable there than by this cold stream."

Suddenly, Gavin heard the birds speak again. One of them said, "Go with her, but give no blood. For if you do, all will be lost."

So Gavin followed the Witchmaiden to a beautiful castle. There they ate from dishes of the finest gold and drank from goblets of pure silver. And then Gavin was shown to a splendid room, where he slept well through the night.

The next morning the Witchmaiden said, "As you can see, I am young and beautiful, and I shall remain so because I have found the secret of the stream. Stay with me—become my husband— and I will share my wealth with you."

But Gavin had not forgotten his search for the magic ring. So he said, "Such an important matter cannot be decided too quickly."

"Of course," the Witchmaiden replied. "Take as long as you like. In the meantime, let me show you around my palace."

And so she took Gavin through each of the magnificent rooms of the palace. Soon they came to a small chamber. And on a silver table stood a tiny golden box.

"This is my greatest treasure," said the Witchmaiden. "It is a magic ring. When we marry, I shall give it to you as a wedding present. And as your present to me, I ask for only three drops of blood from the little finger of your left hand."

Gavin's body went cold as he remembered the warning of the bird. To hide his fear, he asked, "What is so special about this ring?"

"Even I do not understand the power of this magic ring," said the Witchmaiden, "for I cannot read the message on it. But it works great wonders. When I place the ring on the little finger of my left hand, I can fly like a bird. When it is on the fourth finger of my left hand, I become invisible to all. When the ring is on the middle finger of my left hand, nothing can touch me. When the ring is worn on my forefinger, I can build anything I wish in a moment. And when the ring is worn on my thumb, my hand becomes so strong that it can break through rock. I do not know why this is so, but all I say is true."

Gavin knew that this was the magic ring that he had been searching for. He looked at the Witchmaiden and began to shake his head, saying, "I cannot believe the ring has all the powers you describe."

"I will show you," said the Witchmaiden, who was annoyed at being doubted. She put the ring on the fourth finger of her left hand, and immediately she became invisible. Then she put the ring on her middle finger and asked Gavin to reach out toward her. He reached out, but his hand suddenly stopped in midair, as if he had hit a stone wall.

The Witchmaiden laughed. "You see," she said. "It is as I told you."

"It is indeed a magic ring," said Gavin. "But it is magic only when it is worn by *you*. It would not work if *I* wore it."

Unsuspecting, the Witchmaiden handed him the magic ring. He slipped it on the fourth finger of his left hand. Immediately, he became invisible.

"It works for you, too," said the Witchmaiden. "I cannot see you at all. Now take off the ring and become visible again."

Gavin removed the ring but slipped it quickly

on the little finger of his left hand. He became as a bird and flew into the sky.

"What are you doing?" cried the Witchmaiden. "Come back at once!"

Gavin only flew higher.

"Come back," the Witchmaiden shouted. "You have deceived me!"

But Gavin flew still higher into the sky. He did not stop flying until he reached the magician who had taught him the language of the birds.

"I have the ring," said Gavin. "Please tell me what it says."

It took the magician a long time to read the message. But at last he said to Gavin, "Here is what you must do to kill the terrible Dragon. Make an iron horse with wheels under its feet. Then fashion a long, thick spear. In the middle of the spear fasten two strong chains. You must ride the horse to the Dragon and thrust the spear through its jaw. Then quickly fasten the ends of the chain into the ground. The powers of the magic ring will help you to do all this. After three days, the monster will be exhausted—but it will not be dead. You must put the ring on your fourth finger so that you will be invisible. Then you can walk right up to the Dragon and slay it."

Gavin thanked the magician, put the ring on his little finger, and flew back to his own land.

Then, using the magic ring, he built the iron horse and spear and chains—just as the magician had described them. And then he waited.

Soon the terrible Dragon appeared. It was so terrifying that Gavin turned pale. His blood ran cold, but he held his spear steady as the Dragon advanced.

Fire poured from its nostrils, scorching the ground. The Dragon's great tail lashed angrily, knocking down trees as it whipped from side to side. Then, as the Dragon came nearer, Gavin hurled the spear into its hideous jaws. At once, he jumped from his horse and drove the chains into the ground. The monster was chained, but not beaten. It fought so hard to get free that the earth shook as though a hundred quakes were splitting the ground. Mountains trembled and fell. Rivers changed their course. Finally, after three days, the great Dragon was quiet. Gavin quickly put the magic ring on his fourth finger and became invisible. Then he rode up, quickly put the ring on his thumb, and killed the Dragon.

There was great rejoicing throughout the land. Then the King said to Gavin, "What are your three wishes? I shall grant them all."

"First," said Gavin, "I wish this magic ring to be returned to the Witchmaiden, for it is hers."

"Done," said the King.

"Second," said Gavin, "I wish the magician who helped me to be made official Wizard of the Land."

"Done," said the King. "And what is your third wish?"

"I wish," said Gavin, glancing at the King's lovely daughter, "I wish for the hand of the Princess in marriage."

And so, Gavin and the Princess were married in great splendor, and the King made Gavin a Prince. The Prince and the Princess lived together happily for the rest of their days.

The Boy Who Fooled the Dragon

Once upon a time there was a man who had two sons. As will sometimes happen, the sons did not get on well together. The younger son was handsome and good natured. And the older son was jealous.

As the sons grew older, things grew worse. Their father became so tired of their quarreling that he ordered them out of the house. So the two young men began to walk through the woods. They shouted insults at each other and generally behaved in an impolite manner.

Suddenly, the older son seized his brother and tied him to a tree. Then he walked back to their house. He hoped that would be the end of him.

But the young man, whose name was Larick, was clever as well as handsome. As it happened, a stout old peddler walked past the tree. Seeing Larick all tied up, the peddler asked, "Why are you tied to that tree, my son?"

"For a cure," said Larick in a flash. "I was once so fat I could not walk. But this tree has cured me, and now I am thin and strong."

"My word," said the old peddler. "Do you

suppose you could tie me to that tree and help me?"

"If you will but untie my bonds," said Larick, "I will see to it right away."

So Larick tied the old man to the tree. And then he went off, leaving the peddler to think about how he had been tricked.

That was but the first of Larick's clever tricks. Soon his cleverness made him famous throughout the land. The King heard about him, and said, "I am curious about this young man who can outwit everyone. Find him and bring him to me."

So the King's guards brought Larick before the King.

"As punishment for your tricks and pranks," said the King, "I should have your head. However, I will spare you on one condition. There is a great Dragon on the other side of the wood. It is said that the Dragon has a flying horse. Bring the horse to me. If you fail, I shall chop you up in a thousand pieces."

"Very well," said Larick, "you shall have it."

So Larick went straight to the Dragon's stable. And there he found the flying horse eating some hay. But just as Larick reached for the rope to lead the horse away, the animal gave a loud whinny. Now it happened that the Dragon was taking his afternoon nap in the room right above the stable.

"What is going on down there?" roared the Dragon.

Again the horse whinnied, and again the Dragon roared, "What is going on?"

When the horse whinnied a third time, Larick hid behind a pile of hay in the corner. The Dragon came down into the stable breathing fire and smoke. But he could see nothing except the horse. Annoyed at having his nap interrupted, the Dragon gave the horse a sharp beating and went back upstairs.

This time when Larick reached for the rope, the horse did not make a sound. Larick leaped upon his back and galloped off.

The King was astonished when Larick returned with the flying horse. "I will spare your life if you do one more thing for me," he said.

"That is most unfair, your Highness," Larick declared. "You told me that I would be spared if I brought you the flying horse."

"Never mind that," said the wicked King. "To save your life, you must now bring me the covering that lies on the Dragon's bed. If you fail, I shall chop you into a thousand pieces."

"Very well," said Larick. "You shall have it."

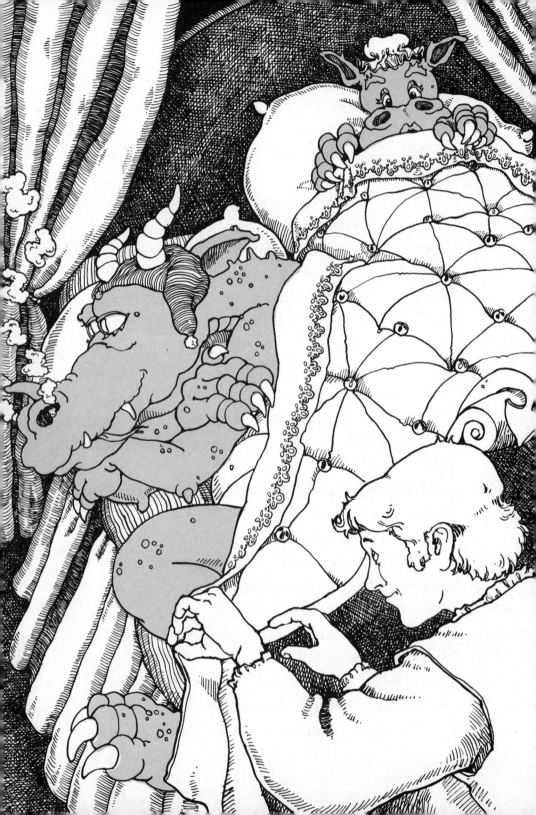

So Larick went to the Dragon's house late that very night. The Dragon and his wife were asleep, so Larick crept into the bedroom and slowly began to pull the cover off the bed. But the cover was filled with little bells that began to jingle. The Dragon woke up and roared at his wife, "You are pulling the cover from me!"

"Not at all," said the Dragon's wife. "I see a youth at the foot of the bed. He is pulling the cover from you."

With that, the Dragon sprang up and seized Larick. He tied him tightly with strong rope and then went back to bed.

In the morning, the Dragon said to his wife, "I must go out to attend to business. When I return, have this youth cooked and ready for eating." And with that, he went away.

The Dragon's wife began to boil some water. But when she untied Larick and tried to put him into the pot, he pushed her in instead! Then Larick snatched the bed covering and brought it to the King.

"You have done well," said the wicked King. "But it is still not enough. I must have the Dragon himself. If you do not bring him to me, I shall chop you into a thousand pieces."

"If I bring back the Dragon, you must promise me one thing," said Larick. "You must give me your daughter's hand in marriage."

"It is agreed," said the King, for he believed that Larick could never bring back the Dragon.

Larick went off into the forest. In time, he grew a beard that was full and bushy and deep red in color. Now the Dragon would not recognize him, so Larick was ready to capture the beast.

Dressing himself in the clothes of a beggar, he traveled to the house of the Dragon once more. There he found the huge, green monster hammering on a box.

"Kind sir, could you spare me a morsel of bread?" said Larick to the Dragon.

"Well, you look hungry enough," said the Dragon. He was thinking to himself that the beggar might make a fine meal. "If you will wait until I have finished making this box, I will find some food for you."

"What are you going to do with that box you are making?" asked Larick.

"I have long been hunting the evil one who has cooked my wife and stolen my flying horse and magic bed cover," said the Dragon. "When I find him, I shall put him in this box."

"An excellent idea," Larick agreed, "for that is what he deserves. However, that box is much too small for him. I have heard he is a large person."

"You are wrong," said the Dragon. "This box would even hold *me*, and a Dragon is bigger than any mortal."

"Well, if *you* can get in it, of course *he* can, too," said Larick. "But, I believe the fit will be too tight."

Now Dragons cannot stand to be corrected. The Dragon's nostrils began to breathe fire. "The fit will not be too tight," he roared in a loud, angry voice. "And I will prove it."

With that, the Dragon jumped right into the box. And true enough, it fit him well.

"I see you are right," said Larick. "But I do not think that the cover will fit on the box with you inside."

The Dragon breathed more fire than ever and became angrier still. "Just put on the cover and you will see," he roared. "I am an excellent carpenter, and I know what I say."

"Very well," said Larick. "We shall see." Larick picked up the wooden cover and put it over the box. "It seems to fit," he said to the Dragon. "But if you push against it, surely it will fall off."

"You are a dunce!" screamed the Dragon. "This cover is made to fit as tight as a drum." The Dragon pushed with all his might. And true enough, the cover of the box remained closed and tight.

"You see," the Dragon shouted from inside the box. "I am right!" He sounded quite pleased with himself. "Now open the box."

But instead of opening the box, Larick picked up a hammer and nails, and nailed the cover tighter still. Then he took the box back to the King.

The King could not believe his eyes when Larick, in his bright red beard, carried the huge box into the throne room.

"Are you sure the Dragon is inside?" asked the wicked King.

"Naturally, I expect that your Majesty will check for himself," said Larick. And he placed the box upon the floor.

First, the King listened to the sounds coming from inside the box. The Dragon was still very angry. Then the King pulled out the nails and lifted one end of the cover to peer inside.

In one snap, the King disappeared into the Dragon's mouth!

Then, Larick married the King's daughter and became the new King of the land. He and his Queen lived happily ever after. And what he did with the Dragon, no one is quite certain. Some say that the Dragon returned to his home, growing quite grumpy in his later years. Others say that he stayed at the castle, where he became good friends with the King and Queen. It all happened a long time ago, and no one knows for sure.